Buckley is a busy boy!

He likes to sleep with his toy.

At night
he cries if it's too dark.

WOOF

Sometimes you may hear him bark.

When he wakes, there is a giant yawn.

Buckley knows it is almost dawn.

Its morning! Its morning! it's time to go.

He stretches his legs, so he can grow.

He gives his family's blanket a tiny tug.

Mom and Dad wake up!
He's ready for a great big hug.

His tail begins to wag
very fast!

Let's go!
Let's go!
Let's not be last!

Buckley is ready for a new day.

He is ready to go outside and play.

But not before breakfast,
wait what will he eat?
A big bowl of cereal
or kibble flavored meat?

Hurry, hurry!

Buckley wants to go outside and play.

He begins to eat so fast just to start the day.

Slow down little buddy
his mom will say...
You will have plenty time
to go outside and play.

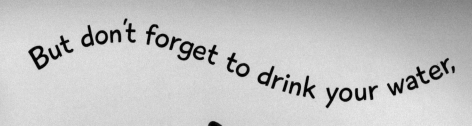

But don't forget to drink your water,

he sighs very loud.

He thinks he saw
a rainy cloud.

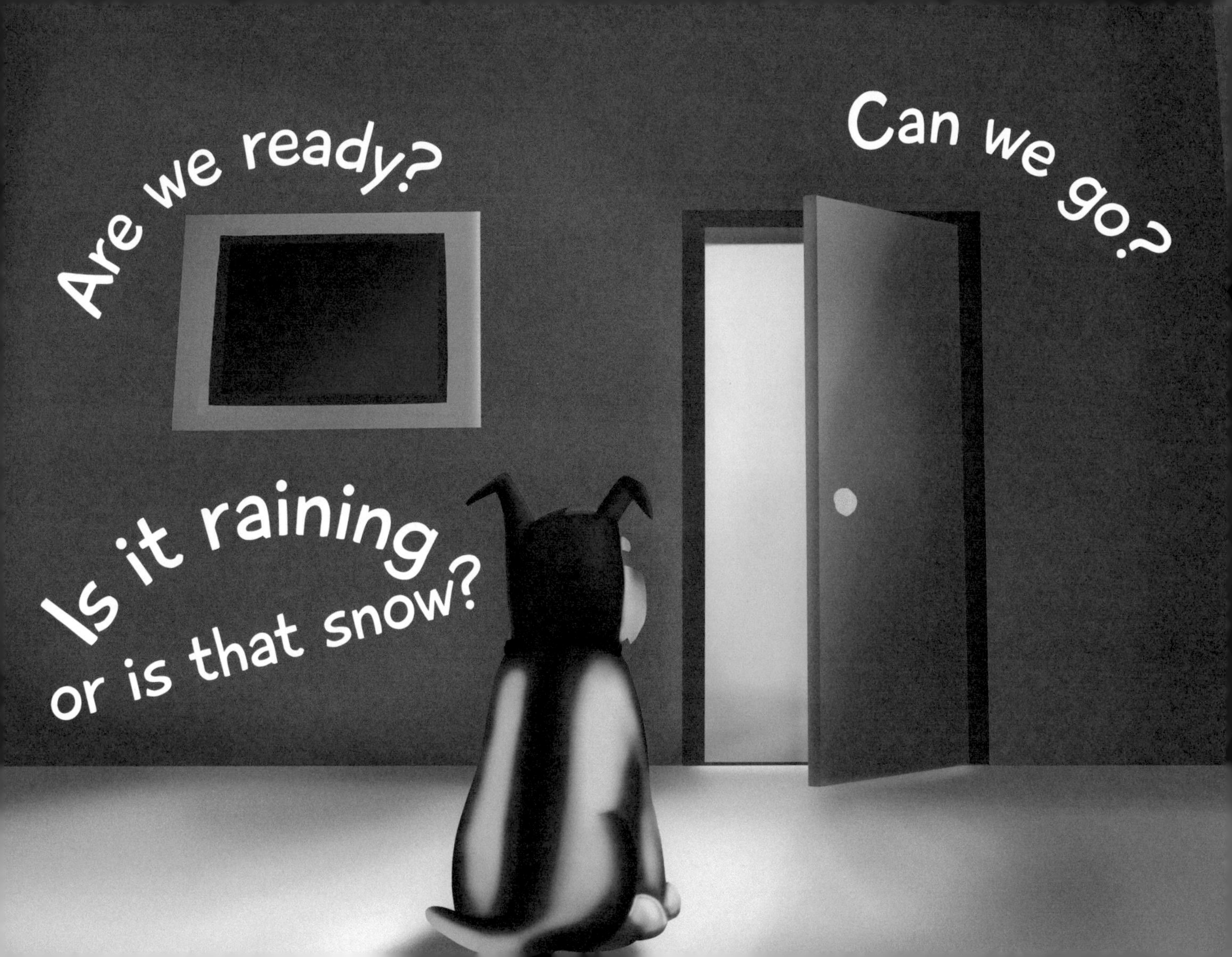

Are we ready?

Can we go?

Is it raining
or is that snow?

No, it's sunny, little buddy

and there is so much to do.

Now, let's go find sticks,

you can chew.

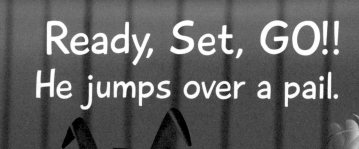

Ready, Set, GO!!
He jumps over a pail.

Buckley is so excited, that he begins to wag his tail.

He chases the chipmunks and squirrels up the trees.

Along with the butterfly, birds, and bees.

But where is the bone he buried yesterday?

Buckley buried it near the ball so he could play.

Dig, dig got to find it,
was it here?
was it there?
Big holes in the backyard are now everywhere!

there is his ball.

Oh, there is his bone,

Now it's time to play with them all.

Yummy, that was good, he lays on his back.

Oh, mom or dad can I have another snack?

No, no its time for bed. Tomorrow we will play.

But for now,

we will say Good Night
and pray
for another day!

The End.

Author's Bio

Susan H. Hines is the author of a children's book series, based on the adventures of her beloved Standard Schnauzer, affectionately named "Buckley." She uses the connection with Buckley to explore his natural learning capabilities and intelligence. Through her observations, she bridges the gap between early readers and their inquisitive nature. She recognizes the unique connections between humans and their furry companions; and the levels of enjoyment they share. Susan H. Hines lives in the Southeastern region of the United States of America with her husband, Edward, and their Standard Schnauzer, Sir Winston Buckley. She received her bachelor's degree in Business Administration from the University of Miami, Coral Gables, FL. Her goal is "to plant trees, she will never see."

Made in the USA
Columbia, SC
18 March 2024

33000658R00018